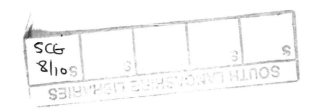
For Charlotte, thanks for all your love
(and all your great ideas!). . . x x
~ T C

For my nephew and godson Nick,
for all your adventures to come
~ A E

LITTLE TIGER PRESS
An imprint of Magi Publications
1 The Coda Centre, 189 Munster Road, London SW6 6AW
www.littletigerpress.com

First published in Great Britain 2010

Text copyright © Tracey Corderoy 2010
Illustrations copyright © Alison Edgson 2010
Tracey Corderoy and Alison Edgson have asserted their rights
to be identified as the author and illustrator of this work under
the Copyright, Designs and Patents Act, 1988

A CIP catalogue record for this book is available from the British Library

Printed in China

LTP/1400/0050/0410

2 4 6 8 10 9 7 5 3 1

Star Friends

Tracey Corderoy

Alison Edgson

LITTLE TIGER PRESS
London

Ooogle-Doogle woke up and peeped
under the bed, just like he did *every*
morning. He checked inside the cupboard,
then underneath the rug . . .

   "*Phew* – no scaries here!" he smiled.
And off he went for breakfast.

Ooogle-Doogle ate a nice plate of blips –
just like he did *every* morning.

Then it was *playtime* – six minutes
building, and six neatly colouring in!

Next, he went to check his blip plants –
to water and dust them, like always.
But just as he polished
his very last leaf . . .
Crunch!
The blip leaves gave a
twitch and *suddenly* . . .

"**Boo!**" cried a scary, munchy thing
with a mouthful of blips! It blew
Ooogle-Doogle a *big, wet kiss* then . . .
"**Boooo!**" cried the Boogle again.

Boooo!

"*Aaarrggh!*" yelled Ooogle-Doogle.
"*A scary! I knew it!* The scaries are *here*!"
And he dashed into the house to hide.

But the Boogle followed too.

Boooo!

"*Aaarrggh!*" cried
Ooogle-Doogle, folding
himself up small.

But the Boogle *liked* this folding
game, so he folded,

flipped . . .

and rolled . . .

all the way across
the floor!

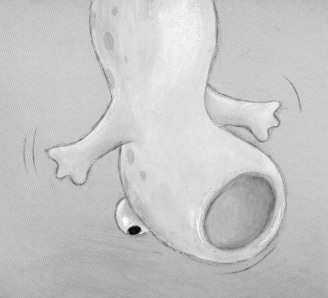

"Boo - boo - boo!"
he chuckled.

Then Ooogle-Doogle began to smile too.

And his smile grew bigger and bigger.

"You're not a scary!" he giggled at last. So he let the Boogle stay.

The next few days passed happily. Ooogle-Doogle taught the Boogle new things, like how to eat blips *neatly* . . .

and how to make *nice, pretty* pictures.

The Boogle taught Ooogle-Doogle things too, like how to water the garden super fast!

As time went on, they made up fun, new games to play together – quiet, careful, cooking games . . .

and racing, chasing, shouty games!

But one day, the Boogle *raced out of the gate!*
"No!" gasped Ooogle-Doogle. He never ever
went out there! What if there were scaries?
But he couldn't let *anything* happen to his
friend, so nervously he followed.

To his surprise, the world outside
the gate was *beautiful*.

He found the Boogle jumping over big bloopies!

"*Be careful!*" Ooogle-Doogle cried.

But it *did* look really fun, so he decided to be brave and have a try.

The Boogle gave him a good luck hug followed by a good luck *prod* . . .

then finally . . .

...boing!

Ooogle-Doogle had done it! And he was
so good at jumping.
"Wheeeeeee!" he cried excitedly.
"I'm flying!"

Then, as he got braver,
Ooogle-Doogle boinged
with the Boogle too!

Up they went and
down they went . . .

Boing!

Wheee!

Doing!

higher and
higher and
higher until . . .

Whoooooooooosh!

the Boogle shot off
Ooogle-Doogle's back
and flew into space!
"Oh no!" cried
Ooogle-Doogle.
"Come back . . ."

But his friend had gone and
Ooogle-Doogle was all alone
once more.

That night he lay under the
stars, high on a hill to be closer
to the Boogle.

"Boo," he sighed. "Night-night,
little Boogle, I miss you!"

Then, all at once, he heard it – echoing down through the sky . . .

BOOOOOOOoooo!

It was the Boogle! He wasn't lost after all. He had landed safely on a star.

"Don't worry!" cried Ooogle-Doogle. "*I'm coming to get you!*"

With that, he boinged with *all his heart* – all the way up to the stars.

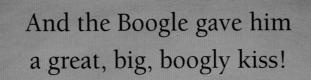

And the Boogle gave him
a great, big, boogly kiss!

From then on, Ooogle-Doogle wasn't
scared of *anything*, for he and the
little Boogle looked after each other.
    And, if you look up on a twinkly night,
you *just* might see them both . . .

. . . boinging about from star to star,
exploring the universe . . .
together!